Illusion: When a Nymphomaniac Falls in Love

Rowan Knight

Published by 22 Lions Bookstore, 2016.

Table of Contents

Title Page

Illusion: When a Nymphomaniac Falls in Love
By Rowan Knight
Copyright © Rowan Knight, 2019 (1st Ed.) All Rights Reserved.
Published by 22 Lions Bookstore and Publishing House

About the Publisher

About the 22 Lions Bookstore:
www.22Lions.com
Facebook.com/22Lions
Twitter.com/22lionsbookshop
Instagram.com/22lionsbookshop
Pinterest.com/22lionsbookshop

Introduction

This could be the romance of many people in pursuit of true love. It begins and ends in the common dream of two souls, highlighting the strength of a passion. The letters of both before they met, saved two lives of endless suffering and created the beginning of a great romance, from a love that until then had not been found. But what would happen later, would reveal a storm of passions that took also both in many different directions.

The Mighty Force of Love

We were in June 2009. A group composed of two French couples roams in the night along a mountain in Mexico. Among them is Bianca, a woman near the age of forty, about to marry Luc, a wealthy young man from the south of France.

Bianca isn't truly in love with Luc. She just saw this one opportunity to stabilize her life, because he's rich and has everything she needs and enjoys in life, namely, the luxury and the possibility of traveling all over the world. Naturally, the fact that they aren't in love generates immense arguments. And that night, one more of these discussions starts, and Luc seeks to press Bianca, saying he doesn't trust what she feels for him.

After several exchanges of harsh words between both, and in a fairly lit tone, she responds confessing that she doesn't love him, never did and has never loved anyone, nor will ever love.

At this moment, Bianca's heart, quite accelerated by the discussion, stops beating. She has a stroke on the mountain, and her friends and boyfriend, without anything they can do, panic. For ten seconds she enters a new world as her soul separates from her body.

There are many souls who present themselves in the form of stars, and they approach to receive her.

For the first time, she feels loved and at peace. Death came to embrace her in eternal love.

At this precise moment, on the other side of the Atlantic, in Portugal, a man makes a wish to the universe. He writes on a paper that he wants to find his soul mate, the person who will be the woman of his life.

After writing this on a special paper, purchased in the same esoteric shop where he had also obtained the accompanying candle, prayed that this woman would come to his life.

The several minutes that accompanied the prayer, seemed hours stopped in time, such was the degree of his concentration, while reciting as mantras his desires and prayers, driven by what more sensitive and profound existed in his intimate.

At this very moment, Bianca comes back to life, in a suffocation of who seemed almost drowned forever in grief, but has just been withdrawn by a higher energy from those deep waters.

After recovering from the fright, Bianca never again was the same. Days later, she suspended her marriage, stating that she needed time to rethink the relationship and which destiny to take in her life, especially after everything that had happened on that mountain in Mexico.

Now in France, she approached the sea with a paper and followed the advice that a psychic had given her years before. Tired of living an empty life, wrote in this paper what she most wished for the future, without fearing to fetch her innermost desires at the bottom of her heart. Much of what she wished for, was something she had lost hope of having: finding love. She wrote that she wanted to find someone she would love with all her heart and that loved her back, she also wrote that she wanted to find someone who would complete her and, in a desire to redeem herself from a lifetime of suffering, she wished to find someone who could heal her, solving all her karmic problems.

A few days after placing the wish in writing, Bianca receives a proposal to work in Changchun, China.

The letters of two people, both still strangers, saved two lives of endless suffering and created the beginning of a great romance, from a love that until then had not been found. The man who saved her was me, and I would eventually and soon meet her there.

The Rebirth to a New Life

Some say death is the beginning of a new cycle. For me, that cycle had come to an end. I remember the day I moved to what only I could call home: A small studio, just with a room for the bed and a bathroom, on top of a building, next to the attic of many other residents. We could even call attic to this space, since it legally didn't possess the conditions to assume the status of a home, or studio, or whatever it was.

This little space in Lisbon was the one I chose to die. I had nothing else to aspire for my life. On the one hand, I had gotten everything I wanted, but on the other hand, there was nothing. I was recognized in my country as the best DJ. But what did I get with this success? Not a penny. Or at least not more than what you could spend on two meals. It was not a field that would generate money and I was essentially a pioneer in what I was doing, namely by mixing opera and classical music in general with extremely fast techno sounds. My performances were more artistic, to amaze and give things to talk about than dancing parties. I did make, for sure, many enemies who wanted to kill me, for envy of the rapid success I had struck, accompanied, I admit, of my immense pride, that in a way I've always considered justified. After all, I wasn't only successful as I also helped other artists get the same. My team was always immensely protected by me.

The hatred, the rage, the fear, the anxiety, and all the other feelings that accompanied me in that time were transported to my performances. The quality was such that success spoke for itself. In the following days, after each performance, many people spoke of the unusual mixtures with the fastest of Japanese sounds, accompanied by mantras or political speeches and voices of films, which have always come at the right time to say something that I wanted to free from the bottom of my heart to the rest of the world: "Want to die? Die with me! Yes, this world has nothing. Accompany me to other universes, where the spirit can fly into infinity and you can be yourself in total freedom. Hate, fear, free yourselves, be happy, be who you are... but live freely!"

For me freedom of speech is as important as the water I drink daily and that was the message that my music conveyed in a powerful but yet aggressive sound, warlike and, at certain times, also of tremendous peace. My inspiration came from the tribal sounds of the Native Americans. A small group acted on the street at night near the place where I was going to DJ. A happy coincidence that promoted my spiritual freedom, in compensation for drugs I've always refused to take, and chocolates that, as antidepressants, destroyed my teeth and my bank account with scamming dentists.

To live the nostalgia of the night and the insignificance of the days, thus I survived as a vampire who only wishes a stake unpredictably coming from the hands of someone. An the anxiety of dying was so great that it always exploded in me when someone was insulting. The neighbors feared me, and those who tried to frighten me too. Collected in the dark, such idiots there appeared at my parties to dance hidden in the corner of the dance floor, hoping maybe that I did not see them and punch them in the face.

There was a lot at stake. I couldn't do it. It could ruin my image, my parties, the reputation of the establishment that was made available to me, the reputation of the owner, etc. This was a vicious cycle that self-destructed me from the inside out.

The money from these events wasn't enough. I had to work during the day as a security guard and also on the nights I didn't DJ. This is where my livelihood came from, for a meaningless life. My life was to get off work and lay on the couch. I refused a bed, a table to eat, and refused to cook. I was just sleeping on this couch when I came in the morning from work. Then I would wake up late, wander to the seaside and come home at the end of the day, with a large void in my chest.

Friends, I was never good at keeping them. Girlfriends, I've never been good at accepting them. I despised others as much as I despised myself. All I wished for was death, because my life wouldn't allow me to create meanings.

Without plans to live a dignified life, I decided to prepare myself to die. I packed all my stuff in boxes. I threw in the trash what I didn't need to use anymore. And I basically sought to limit my existence to the essentials: my laptop and the couch to sleep. This, in a tiny space on the roof of a huge building, a windowless attic where the smell of death increased before the absence of hope to live.

However, on the night of my 30th birthday, when I came home and opened the email, I saw the best birthday gift I could get. I got the invitation from a university in China to be a teacher. An offer that I had no idea exactly where it came from, because it had been almost a year since, in desperation, I decided to send several resumes by e-mail to every corner of the world.

I was now ready to take a leap in the void, to surrender myself completely in the hands of God, whether He was or not bluffing with me.

I still recall the moment when the plane took off from the runway and my heart flitted from the impurities of a miserable, hopeless and loveless life. I seemed to be waking up from a coma. It was a moment of tremendous joy, as my country grew increasingly, and was small among clouds at the same time.

In heaven, I was in God's hands. He had handed me the desired death, so I could go to a new life.

For the two nights preceding this trip, I received flashbacks of my entire life, of what I had lost and what I had exceeded successfully. A divine message about the state of my karma.

The night before, I was still on a prep trip, where I dreamed I was alone on a huge airplane. I was finally in God's hands, because we can't play as much with him as we can play for him.

Totally in the clouds, in divine hands, I died to be reborn. I got the death I wished for, but I was reborn in the same body. This was the beginning of a new journey.

When Stability Prevents Opportunities

Three planes and 24 hours later, I was in China for the first time. Small houses by agricultural fields certainly weren't descriptive of my homeland, where homes pile up as if all people wished each other ardently, which is indeed not the case.

I was feeling very, but really, very well. My life was about to restart. I was happy in the midst of so much confusion, with so many people around me talking a language that I knew nothing about, observing Chinese ads everywhere, and everything else that made me believe I had reached another planet.

The arrival at the destination airport didn't go as well as expected. I lost a suitcase on the way that later knew had stayed in Beijing. Waiting for me, I had two staff from the university where I was going to work. I had a feeling I was being transported by some kind of mafia organization. Both sitting in the front, little or no English they spoke. Even when I was trying to talk something, they seemed not to understand English.

The distance traveled was long, but I finally got there. The apartment I was provided with was huge, bigger than I imagined. Only the living-room was bigger than my entire old apartment. Inside the fridge, I found cookies and bananas that well fell into my stomach because I had nothing to eat that night. It was late and everything was closed. The enormous and empty, clean and pure house of so new it was, was, without a doubt, made to receive me.

It was late, and so I soon laid to sleep in the kingsize bed. I haven't slept in a bed for years, but more than anything, I haven't felt peaceful in my sleep for many years too. That night, I really rest my spirit, as a new soul that had just traveled to a new birth.

In the following morning, one of the employees came to my apartment to greet me. I felt truly important and respected and my joy was impossible to conceal. I was accompanied to the University secretariat where, then accompanied by another of the employees, I was invited to see the whole college campus. I was fascinated with both gardens and trees and, above all, the tranquility. To me, it was like I had died and entered paradise. I was all very peaceful.

When I was asked, after being escorted through the campus, if I was interested in signing the contract, I didn't hesitate to answer yes. And, hours later, I met the director of my department, as well as his colleague. I found a little intimidating the many questions that the director made me in the ever-friendly tone, about my work experience, as well as the thorough analysis made on my competences. This was for me as odd as the fact that the other teacher didn't want to say anything. But I was in China, a country I knew nothing about. So neither the fact that they didn't have a teaching program with the subjects foreseen to teach bothered or caused strangeness in me. I was happy and everything seemed great.

The next day, I met the Italian teacher. He walked like an alien from a sci-fi film and had a face resembling a goblin from The Lord of the Rings, with his big eyes and pointed nose. I got a fright at first, but talked amicably with him, reporting my fears, yearnings and needs. He showed himself understanding and passive. He was made available to introduce me to other teachers and to direct me around the city to shop. Shortly thereafter I was shopping with the Spanish, Chilean and Italian teachers, my earliest friendships.

The Spaniard had a very interesting appearance, but it was not very enthusiastic about meeting me. Later I came to know that she suffered from some kind of psychological complex. She had difficulties in trusting men. But is there a woman who doesn't?

When we arrived, since I was in a bigger and farther apartment, without information about the Chinese lessons in the university, had to go back to the block of apartment buildings for foreign teachers to check the classroom hours. There were four different doors and, for reasons that only in my intuition I can find the answer, I chose door number two, at that precise moment.

I was observing the paper when something in me ordered me to wait. After a few seconds, the door opened, and Peppe, the Italian teacher, came in, accompanied by another teacher. Something about her trapped my attention and made me feel dumb.

-Hi David, this is Bianca, a French teacher!, said Peppe in a friendly tone.

-Hi!, I answered, without knowing what to say next.

-Hello, you live here?, she answered happily.

-No! I live with the Chinese teachers because my Chinese is excellent!, I told her.

-Seriously?, questioned her intrigued by my joke.

-No!, I replied between laughters.

Suddenly, it seemed to me that she didn't realize my ironic tone, and didn't like it. Went by me, went up the stairs, but unexpectedly turned back and asked: -Do you want to come to my apartment?

Peppe was surprised and I even more. I didn't know what to answer. I wonder if we were in love. I wasn't sure and I couldn't be. I answered something like...

-Maybe next time!

I think my state of shock was such that I couldn't be sure of the words I used. All I know is that from that day on, my life had change completely because I thought about her all the time. All I wanted to do was go shopping with the teachers and Peppe, the Italian, for obvious reasons.

The first time we started changing words in the supermarket, I asked Peppe, well-known about the Chinese culture, if he knew where I could buy goji berries. And he replied that he didn't know what it was, but Bianca answered immediately: -I know where to find it!

She took me with her and I could see that her enthusiasm towards me was as big as mine for being with her. I was just more afraid of demonstrating it. We were both completely in love, without a doubt. It was an obvious fact to both but doubted by both as well. Would such strong attraction be real? This was our most common thought.

The next day I got a call from her: -Peppe will organize a dinner for us. Do you want to go with me buy the wine?

-Yes!, I answered without hesitating for a second.

-I can go alone, too, I don't care and maybe it's better!, she answered, using my lack of confidence against me to test me.

I wanted to be with her so much that I didn't think of anything else and said right away: -I know a lot about wine!, which wasn't true, as I don't even drink.

At the party, I ended up being unmasked, even though she didn't realize before that moment, while we were shopping.

During dinner, I couldn't take my eyes off her. The confident way she walked, her curves, her sensual and sexy eyes, all that made me completely mad. I tried to keep my composure but it was difficult and sometimes I had to disguise I was watching her as a starving lion.

In the next days I noticed she avoided me, maybe because she was afraid of her feelings. But I always tried to be close when Bianca talked to someone.

The First Encounters

My washing machine was very prehistoric and, in conversation with other teachers in the group, I said I didn't understand how that machine works. To what Bianca replied that I could use her machine.

Perfect, so I thought. An opportunity to spend time together falling from the sky, or more properly from her mouth. The Chilean teacher said afterwards that I could also use her machine but, between the woman of my dreams and a Chilean grumpy old enough to be my mother, or more than that, the choice was certainly obvious, although I was embarrassed by the fact that I had to choose and the enjoyment of Bianca by forwarding me to Chilean.

Bianca had certainly realized that I felt sexually attracted to her, and she used it now to create a game with me and make herself difficult to get. However, as I didn't call her, trying to win the game she created, she called me that same night, and I finally got into her territory.

As the laundry washed, we sat down to drink tea and talk, but I confess that I felt intimidated, because there was something about her that fascinated me completely. When I sat down, I chose the opposite corner of the couch where she snuggled. I was watching her intrigued while we were talking, trying to figure out what was going on with me. Meanwhile, the conversation was flowing so well that we rotated the timer on the machine several times.

-Maybe the clothes aren't washed yet!, she said sometimes. -We better restart the process!

For three nights in a row of laundry and conversations in the middle, she told me she was very fond of talking to me, because I was the only person she could talk to about all sorts of things. And the more time we spent together, the more time I wanted to be with her, the more I wished her, the more I wanted to kiss her. We started to find all sorts of pretenses to meet and go out together, just the two of us and not with our group. But we weren't prepared for a new relationship, and especially not so fast. We had just arrived China three weeks before. The emotional tension and the fact that we both wished for this relationship, while we were afraid to accept it, was always present. Nevertheless, we were going to gardens and restaurants like two lovers.

During these moments when we were dating, I was checking in on her behavior somewhat odd. She was extremely interested in me, but at the same time seemed to be afraid of the consequences, fear of liking someone. One day I tried to talk to her about it but without great success. She didn't like the conversation. Fortunately, however, it didn't affect the relationship and we continued going out together.

One day we were talking about her experiences in Mexico when I told her I had given personal defense lessons in the past. She was enthusiastic and interested in learning. She said no one ever taught her. And so, we arranged for a day at the end of the afternoon, out of class hours, in my apartment, because it was much more spacious.

Although I ended up forgetting this promise, she reminded me later, and we had the class. She came to my apartment dressed in the worst possible way, with a black tracksuit, old tennis and with a messed hair, perhaps to discourage me from trying to teach more than some street techniques.

Despite my professionalism in what I was doing, our proximity, being eyes in the eyes, began to accentuate even more what already existed. When I grabbed her hands, to teach some defensive locks, it flowed into me an energy that came directly into my brain. If there were doubts before, they had been dissipated in that moment. At the end of the workout we stopped to drink water, and when she said: -It's time to go!, I felt I didn't want her to leave me anymore. -Don't go! I have something important to tell you!, I said to her.

She seemed scared about it and insisted on leaving, but I continued: -Don't go, because I have to tell you this now!

When the words started coming out of me, Bianca wrapped herself of so intimidated she felt. And while she was sitting, I confessed to her that I loved her, and I couldn't continue without her. -I fall asleep thinking about you, I wake up thinking about you, and I'm all day thinking about you. And I've never felt this way about anyone before, which is why I felt so confused about what was going on between us. When you're near me, I feel different, my heart beats faster and I feel nervous, like I've never felt near a woman before!

Bianca had no words to answer, and began to weep while seeking to conceal her hands with the face: -I think I should leave! But, thank you!, she answered me, moved.

Although I felt disappointed with her attitude, I was also tired of so much gambling, and satisfied with myself for putting the cards on the table and make it clear for the first time. I felt a mixture of relief with disappointment inside me, and so I let her go.

-Did you lock the door?, she asked while desperately trying to open it.

The question and the attitude seemed totally inappropriate. -Well, what a stupid question after what I said!, I told her. I went to the door and opened it immediately, moving away from her right after. But, Bianca approached me to give me a goodbye kiss in the mouth. It didn't look like a kiss from someone who wanted to stay, but more than someone wanting to thank me, so I let her go after that moment.

The Next Day

The next day, Bianca called me, saying she wanted to talk. But as soon as she opened the door, walked away from me, lowering her gaze. I decided to take the initiative and gave her a passionate kiss, which didn't receive great reciprocity. When we sat down to talk, I realized why: -I think we'd better stop here!

-If you don't want this relationship, you'll never see me again!, I replied confused by her attitude, but also revolted with her behavior.

-We can keep seeing each other!, she answered.

-No! If you don't want to assume a relationship with me, I never want to see you again, because it would be too painful for me. Are you sure that's what you want?

-I don't know!, answered Bianca now confused with my reaction.

-You better know, because from this day on, if you don't want the relationship, I'm going out that door and I'm not looking back!, I answered her without any doubt in my words.

She hesitated. -I'm not sure. But then confessed: -I want the relationship, but what if it doesn't work?

-The effort is mutual, and if we love each other I don't see how it wouldn't work. We're always together and well all this time!

Bianca agreed in assuming the relationship, even if we had decided to keep it private, and kissed again. In the next days, we always went out together like two lovers, because all we wanted was to be together. We existed as if we were one person. We talked for hours and hours without end, and the conversations flowed into the most diverse subjects. We also kissed as if we knew each other for hundreds of years, and it seemed like we were building a new form of dialogue with kisses, because they were always different and prolonged. We were like two souls who knew each other thousands of years ago and had reencountered after a long period apart.

The First Discussions

Small arguments began occurring with some frequency, and that started shaking the relationship and my self-confidence. One of those first discussions, for example, resulted from the way I took her and kissed her. She told me I kissed her without emotion and that remark didn't just make any sense but also hurt me. It was as if she was testing my emotional stability and trying to undermine my self-confidence. This behavior of her part made me prepared to get out of the relationship, and that's what I did at the precise moment when I said it, without later answering her phone calls.

The next morning, by email, and already calmer, I expressed myself more clearly:

"Bianca, I tried to make you happy because even I have a hard time at smiling. I can only feel that happiness through you. But if you try to make me someone I'm not, you're following the path of the people that have rejected me in my life. If you reject what I am, you're rejecting me. Don't expect me to feel things I can't feel and don't expect me to stop having abilities that I have. If you don't love the person I am, you don't love me. What you did to me yesterday was a rejection. I love you, but our relationship will never work if you don't love me. I told you the only way to end this relationship is if you decide it like that. I think you're deciding. I still love you very much, and I still wake up thinking about you. Every day that passes, I love you more, but every day that passes, I feel more rejected by you. Think about what you're prepared to accept before you apologize and then make me feel the pain of rejection. I'm not that different from you. In my way, I also live, like you. Love me or reject me."

This email resulted in an apology from Bianca's part, a sincere and dramatic request, while kneeling in front of me and grabbing my hands. And for that reason, I came back to her, thankful for her compassion.

However, it was not long before this situation suffered repercussions because of her anxiety and doubts as to what I felt for her, as on the same day, at night, we argued again due to her behavior. This time, her reaction was opposed to what she had in the morning. And, feeling rejected, but loving her deeply, I sent the following email at night:

"Bianca, today I was dining in the cafeteria, and observed two chefs. One had the flame of the stove very high. The fire would practically rise up to his face. The other had the fire at its minimum. They both finished cooking at the same time. We had problems in just a week, one after the other. The flame of our conflicts was high, but I believe that ultimately the outcome could be the same as these two cooks. I told you I was prepared to keep the flame on, whatever happened, and you promised not to have radical attitudes again. Today I gave you a chance to talk, even if I didn't feel good, but you're not doing the same thing. I don't think you're being wise. I'm not as patient as you. I can't just sit around and watch what happens to us. I won't be able to sleep tonight. I'm doing for you what I've never done for anyone. I'm struggling to maintain the relationship, regardless of how painful this might be to me. I don't want you to fear me or get me out of your heart, there's no reason for that. Let me talk to you! I promise to be brief! I'll wait for your message! Don't be the rock you asked me not to be! I love you!"

Days after this message, she insisted that I move into her apartment. It happened very quickly and I didn't feel prepared to share a house with someone else. Unbelievably, it had only been four weeks since I had arrived in China, and only two weeks since I had seen her for the first time, and I was already living with Bianca, believing to be the woman of my life.

Where the Heart Lives

So much good in a relationship between two people who had suffered enough in life was somewhat baffling, and it was from this contrast with happiness that gradually the stability of the relationship began to be shaken. Bianca was ten years older than me, almost forty, and she felt less stable than me. Her fears quickly seized her mind and slowly the tests to my personality and fidelity began. The first tests were essentially fidelity tests. She was afraid of losing me, and so she tested me the whole time, namely by creating jealousy. She was also afraid that I could be aggressive, and afraid that I would be jealous and restrict her independence, and finally she was afraid that I would abandon or abuse her in some way. Those were a lot of fears for a person who told me she'd always had wonderful boyfriends. It cost me too much to believe. It didn't make sense. Would I be the worst of them all? And if so, why did she say she felt with me what she never felt before? Why was she terrified of losing me and never had that fear before? Her tests were systematic and each more irritating and painful than the previous one. I remember the moment when she switched off my computer's external disk in full operation, knowing that I could lose a lot of important documents, or the moment I was cooking dinner for the two and she told me at the end that she wasn't going to eat because she wasn't hungry, and that she had dinner with a colleague. During those frictions, Bianca didn't seem to be worried about my feelings, but so-only hers. When she saw me hurt, even if I didn't answer her, she would provoke a reaction: -How can you be like that? It's just a burger! Just for a burger with my colleague, you're like this?

A colleague which, in turn, was chasing her for a long time, and didn't know she was with me. Actually, it wasn't just a hamburger. Every time we went to McDonald's, she kept staring at me saying she didn't eat meat from that place. She refused to have lunch or dinner with me at this place but didn't refuse it with a colleague who was interested in her. And finally there's still the fact of knowing that I would cook for her and was waiting for the final moment when everything was ready to tell me. The purpose of annoying me was too explicit. But I think the real purpose was to create jealousy to analyze my reaction. Maybe she wanted to know if I was one more of the many jealous boyfriends she had in the past. It certainly made sense. But why did I have to pay for her troubles? And why would she bring her past into a relationship that flourished like a wonderful flower?

Her fear was successively deteriorating the relationship. But she wouldn't stop here. Like almost in a psychosis, Bianca did a lot worse. She sought everything that could disturb me, systematically analyzing my reactions in a daily basis. I remember, for example, a day we were in a restaurant and an employee wouldn't stop looking at her. At first I showed myself disturbed and she started arguing with me, provoking me: -You're going to have to get used to it! If you start being jealous, you'll definitely lose me!, she told me in a arrogant attitude that I wouldn't allow.

-Well, actually, if you don't look at him too, it's possible he doesn't look at you!

She didn't like the answer but admitted my reason. At that moment, she felt intimidated by me and, as a child in contradiction and spoiled, refused to look at him. In spite of that, two weeks later we came back to this restaurant, and from what it seemed, her vengeance was planned. And as soon as she saw the same employee, said to me with prepotence: -I'm going to talk to that employee, who's my favorite!

I didn't answer this time because the intention was too obvious. Her behaviors became so premeditated that I just started ignoring her. From then on, she started arguing with me because of my silence. I mean, I couldn't be jealous and at the same time I was supposed to be jealous. Not knowing what game was hers, I refused to play it and give her the dominion of my emotions. But she insisted, trying to kiss me when she saw me bored. And, as I refused her advances, she wore this excuse as a reason to end the relationship. It was like, in a very sick way, she needed to feel full dominance over the relationship.

I tried to solve the problem, but she never wanted to admit bad relationships in the past. Always said the opposite, that they were all better than me. However, she admitted that she was provoking me for fear of abandonment, and also admitted that she was afraid of me, for reminding her parents who had abused her as a child.

These confessions, though significant, weren't enough to end the problems. Yes, from that moment on, Bianca has developed another fear, fear of change. She was changing a lot with the relationship and was terrified of the changes. She had become accustomed to her personality, which, despite being a self-destructive personality, was the personality she knew and so she didn't want to lose herself, the self she knew. Her fear of changing, of stopping being as she knew herself, made her refuse to listen to me whenever we had problems, accusing me of trying to manipulate her. From there, she sought to achieve dominance of all problems and discussions and, with this, we passed from two weeks of absolute peace, to moments of increasing destruction. Bianca was letting herself be seized by her fears again. She was creating more discussions, began avoiding me and finally decided to expel me from home.

After begging me to return, these expulsions began to become one of her weapons to demote me every time I had my hand. And such behavior began to affect my emotional stability, probably as she intended, in a very sadistic attitude. Her fears ended up becoming mine too. But it seemed that while I became more unstable, she was becoming increasingly confident towards my lack of confidence.

This situation led me to make a radical decision. I decided to stay two months without seeing her in my country to assess the relationship at a distance. I invented the excuse that I had a lot of issues to resolve and that there would be time to later be together. This was the first time I saw her clearly very afraid of losing me, and it was also the first time she made constant efforts to make me feel good. During the last few weeks before I left, we made love as never and very often daily. And whenever she saw me bothered with something, she would hasten to abdicate her point of view to accept mine. She was very careful all the time and until the day I took the taxi to the airport.

In the morning I had to get the taxi, she was in tears. She had put several candles in the house, and when I woke up, we spent a few hours together before the departure. It was a very intense and dramatic moment. When we said goodbye, I couldn't help feeling that I was saying goodbye to a dream.

When the Past Makes the Future Impossible

When arriving my country, now away from Bianca, I began to recall all of our conversations differently. I remembered the many conversations when she told me she had sex with an immense amount of men for many years and from a very early age. The pride she felt by saying this made me feel like I was dating a hooker or at least a nymphomaniac. Then I started remembering the jealousy games she created, the mockery she was doing to my behavior and my personality. All of a sudden, all these memories started to fit, and I got the idea that I wasn't with a normal woman, but a sexual pervert that was playing with me. I couldn't talk to her during this period. She, in turn, sensing that something went wrong, called me countless times a day and without stopping, until I finally had to answer the phone: -You have to change! You have to stop hurting me and saying goodbye all the time!, I said.

-What do you want me to do? You want me to kill myself to prove that I love you?, she said in an angry tone.

-I just want you to promise that you're going to change your behavior.

She agreed, but I didn't know if I could believe her word. After this incident, I decided not to call until she called me, which only happened in the fifth day: -Why didn't you call me?

-I was wondering if you'd call me after what happened!

-Oh, you were testing me like an animal!, she replied irritated.

-No, I just didn't know what to say!

Bianca decided to charge for this attitude, avenging herself once again: -I had a heart problem because of you and I spent the last five days in the hospital. I was always waiting for you to call me and you never did. You know what, It's all over for me! I don't want this relationship anymore!

This said, she turned off the call. After that, whenever I called her, she said she was in the presence of friends and having fun. But her constant confident tone as if provoking me, let me think that she would be initiating a new relationship, or perhaps returning to an old relationship. And I started preparing for the fact that I lost her.

In search of the truth about what was really happening, I searched for two psychics, to confirm their responses. A psychic, already very old, told me she was playing with me like I was a toy. She said Bianca had mental disorders and used her manipulations to control me, but didn't really like me. She said Bianca thought she was winning, but she was going to lose. She also said we'd both meet other people. In the case of her an older man and in my case a younger woman. But she wouldn't succeed, because she would find a man who would control her, and I would succeed, finding someone who would help me.

Actually, the colleague who was always after her was older than her. And according to the second psychic, a middle-aged gentleman, she was raising discussions because she was already cheating on me.

I tried to understand this story better with the help of a friend psychologist. This one helped me realize that I was manipulated and that Bianca didn't really love me. She helped me realize that her excess of confidence, and the lies she propagated all the time, were a clear sign of someone who's playing and manipulating, but doesn't really like me. Then I decided to stop calling her for more than two weeks to become clearer about the situation. I had accepted destiny as it was. But the same thing didn't happen to Bianca, who started suffering from panic attacks. She started calling me dozens of times a day without stopping and sent several messages saying she was suffering.

I didn't understand this sudden panic, but I had no reason to answer either. I never answered or responded to any messages, but Bianca, now terrified of losing me forever, phoned without stopping for several days.

When I got the plane back to China, I was different. No more was the same man in love with a lunatic. I still loved her, but I was relearning mainly to love myself.

Home is Where We Are

I came by surprise on a February night and Bianca didn't expect me. I had to knock on her door, even though it was 22pm, because the key to my apartment and all my things were in her apartment.

I thought I'd bring with me enough courage to face the situation, but in her presence I feel weak. She, in turn, even though in the last few days had been trying to talk to me, didn't falter even a little with my arrival, and seemed very different, very lean and depressed.

I didn't know what to say, while she was taking my stuff and delivering them to my hands. I sat in the end to talk to her, but in a low and weak voice, she told me she didn't want the relationship anymore. So I took all the stuff and went to my apartment, although, after seeing her, I couldn't maintain my willpower anymore.

In my apartment, I couldn't connect the internet, and I called her to ask to open the door for me to get the cable. And when I was going to say goodbye, it all happened again. We stayed together that night. As much as it would cost me to admit, I just felt peaceful with her, not apart. I couldn't resist her.

That peace, however, didn't last long. She was now more irritated and unstable than ever. And I had the feeling that she'd done something I was afraid to find out. We were never together more than two or three days, without her intentionally creating a conflict and feeling unstable, ending the relationship short-after.

Fortunately, after a few weeks had arrived two new teachers from Spain with whom I began to go along with frequently. But I thought it was odd that Bianca was so excited about these, inviting them all the time to her home. Something I ended up learning to use against her. I remember a night that she argued with me and put me out of the house, and then I went to talk to her front neighbor, one of those Spaniards. I was so used to the situation, I ended up having fun with him talking about a lot of things. She, who listened to my laughter, couldn't handle it and spent all night calling me. But I didn't answer. I was asleep already, at 2 A.M., when I woke up with her calls and answered the phone. Bianca was crying and sobbing. I asked her if she wanted to come and talk to me. And I was surprised that she came running and shaking. We spent the night together.

Nevertheless, the fights were still continuous, and sometimes in a very disrespectful manner. Bianca also began to show a very insane behavior because she listened behind the door the conversations I had with her Spanish neighbor. In one of those conversations I had with him, I decided to test what I already suspected for a long time, and I opened the door suddenly, to what Bianca tried to run down the stairs, not getting away in time. She ended up making a childish face when caught in the act and squealed in irritation. I didn't even answer because I could only laugh at her immature and ridiculous behavior. I'd just begin to move away from her, taking advantage of the fact that we haven't lived in the same apartment since I was there. But seeing that I began to move away, Bianca decided to start sending more revealing emails, trying to arouse compassion in me:

"David, I know now that I've disconnected myself from my feelings for a long time. For a long period of my life, unconsciously, I believed that experiencing very extreme situations was the only way to feel anything. Then later, I realized that I put myself in danger many times, just to have a moment of intense emotion that everyone feels but me. Obviously, I had to change this behavior, as it was becoming very risky and unhealthy to live like this. So I decided to switch to a completely opposite strategy for a safer life. I closed myself to any sensation for my own good. The truth is, I became very open to offering people what I was unable to receive. I devoted myself completely to others, seeing this solution as quite comfortable, because I thought I was happy and made the people around me happy too. What I told you before, that you were living in a castle made by yourself so that you couldn't be hurt, is a game I played, though with different rules. In my case, the purpose was not to protect me not to be hurt (to the extent that it is the only feeling that I really and truly experience) but not feel. I thought it was perfect. Then you came into my life, bringing with you a love that I couldn't manifest. A love that I often tried to show without success. With what you are and the feelings you had for me, you dragged every deeper sensation, every memory buried inside me for a long time, and the result is that I completely collapsed. I couldn't recognize the way I was behaving, I didn't recognize my old me. I rejected your love because I couldn't handle it. The feelings we had for each other, the sensations experienced, were so strong that I couldn't deal with this anymore. So, little by little, I put you out of my body, my life, my heart. What you said often, that you were taking great risks in helping me change, sadly, despite your fears, happened. I hope you know I'm sorry I hurt you, but you get this letter as a gift for what you've challenged in you to do for me. For you can see the outcome of your work: Me writing about feelings and being completely honest with myself and with you. I think I'm on the right track for my recovery. I wish one day you can talk to me again without the pain that I put between us."

Although the letter seemed sincere, I knew this time I had to be more attentive, so I kept my silence for weeks, only answering afterwards:

"Bianca, I'm sorry if I hurt you or didn't trust you enough, but it all came from the fear of losing you. The same fear you have about me. It's because we love each other so much that fear exists. It will disappear in time. Perfection doesn't come in a heartbeat. It's built, just like a sculpture. The one who sees beauty can find it in a rock and do something beautiful, because beauty already existed there. We became rocks, but we built the beauty that was inside with our relationship. We don't need to ask for anything from each other because love builds everything for us from what we already have. It's because I can seen beauty inside you that I can love you. Time and life do the rest. These last two weeks have been perfect. It was the fear of losing each other that ruined everything one more time. All I do is to keep your happiness. I know you need me out of your life to find the job you need in the city you want, without any commitment to stop you. I know that's what made you think so much about the relationship in the last few days and saying things that made me feel hurt. And it's because I knew that I avoided you. I want your happiness, but I love you with all my heart, too. So I tried to let you go. I wanted to let you decide for yourself if I was worthy of being a part of your life. Sometimes the pain of respecting your decisions is unbearable, but I do my best. It's because I love you so much that I hurt you. I am sorry. It's not so much about trusting you as the fear of losing. Loving you is a purpose in my existence that brings me more joy than any other, even if that love passes for letting you go."

As if it wasn't enough, every time we argued, I saw her going out with the same colleague. It was always with Barnabas that she had fun. The time she spent with him, whenever she ended the relationship with me, gave me the feeling that she didn't care at all about my feelings. One day, I saw her go out with this colleague at four in the afternoon and cheerfully arriving at midnight with him. When we were together again and I confronted her with the fact that she spent the whole time with this colleague, she answered me: -But at night it's you I sleep with!, and I was still thinking about this assertion and what it really meant. But I also resent the fact that every time I spoke of him, she was annoyed, as if protecting him.

I knew this kind of behavior couldn't last a long time, and sooner or later I'd have to stop seeing her, which could only be possible if changing city. However, she spent the time offering me the opportunity to live with her in another country. My messages to her began to become more fatalistic and insistent in the fact that she should show more honesty, which, in no way, ever happened:

"Bianca, at first you finished the relationship many times and then you apologized. After that you ended several times and came to me crying to keep it. After those moments, you spent two months away from me and treating me like I was trash, saying you didn't want this relationship anymore. Then, afraid I wouldn't come back, you were so afraid of losing me that you'd call me every day. I came back to you because I believed in you and because after all you did, whether I was crazy or not, the fact is I still loved you. In China, again, you've finished the relationship many times. When I started to walk away, you tried to conquer me back. If you didn't get me, you wouldn't eat and you wouldn't sleep. Then you created bigger conflicts this time with physical aggression on your part. But when you realized you could lose me forever, you wanted us to get back together again. Now we have a free week to be together and recover from our past, and you end this relationship on the first day, ironically, after you said you didn't expect anything else and saying you didn't want to let me go, and after you said as well, and I quote: "I want to leave you but I can't."

You can believe I'm analyzing you, while I believe I'm trying to understand you, to be able to see how you want to be loved. As the fights continued, also your motives changed, every time I solved a problem, as if you wanted to keep the war between us.

1st we argued because you were afraid to lose me;

2nd we argued because you think I am ashamed to show an older girlfriend to my family and colleagues;

3rd we argued because I complained about your behaviors all the time;

4th we argued because you believe I want to change you to someone you are not;

5th we argued because you said I can't hear you;

6th we argued because you said that we argued all the time (hmmm... confusing, no?);

7th we argued because I feel insecure in the relationship (and wow, this lasted two months, maybe because you're too afraid to lose me, I believe);

8th we argued because you believe that I am aggressive and I can hurt you (which is very interesting, as you are the one who were physically aggressive, and apparently, from what you told me, it was not the first time you did it to someone);

9th we argue because you say I hurt you with words;

10th we argue because you say that I didn't express myself (what ironically I began to do after you said that I hurt you with words, words that weren't more than me pointing to the way you hurt me);

11th we argued because you said I'm not romantic;

12th we argued because you said I am not affectionate;

13th we argued because you claimed to be unhappy with me;

14th we argued because you were unhappy;

15th and the relationship has become so ridiculous in front of your constant complaints, that you now argue with me when I don't kiss you. But yes, we were very happy. In the days when you believed we could be happy without arguments and dreams were becoming true.

You've seen it many times, but you're so afraid to believe, because for you a relationship is like a war on control and power.

I wonder who the previous idiots in your life were that ruined your brain about loving someone. It's because you're in this game that you're surprised when the outcome doesn't appear as you hoped. Then you think the other person is confusing. But there's no confusion. Only the power play and the dynamics of love are'n't compatible. Loving is giving up power and control, it's respecting someone else. The first day we kissed, you didn't want to kiss me. I appreciate the fact that the door didn't open for the kiss that I didn't want to force. In the second day you wanted to end the relationship.

I'm not judging you because I love you. I know that everyone can make mistakes. I'm not perfect. I can hurt, just like you. I can do a lot of bad things, including without intent, like you. It's normal to make mistakes. And I can also understand that you've had a very difficult life. At the same time, I also understand that it is because your life was so difficult that you learned to survive in a strange way, which allows you to be the best in some things and worse in others. I admire what you've accomplished in your life and I admire your courage in living, dedication to work and willingness to succeed. When I met you, it was like a dream come true. Even better than that, because I was fascinated by the fact that we had a perfect connection. I was very enthusiastic about it, and I let myself into the relationship without thinking twice. I've done for you what I've never done for anyone. Then I saw you use your wits against yourself. I tried to help you, and that help turned against me, as you blamed me for making you feel bad.

I helped myself as much as I could. I've changed so much not to give you any more grief. But if your suffering does not find an explanation in my actions, you find now in my inactions. So if I kiss you but don't ask how the day went, or if I ask but don't kiss you, or ask about today's day but not yesterday, or if I just forget, everything is a valid reason to blame me for your unhappiness. Surprisingly, you even believe that flowers can survive for a whole month with me because they absorb my negative energy and live on it. What to say then about they only surviving less than a week with you? It's surprising how much you change reality to strengthen your needs. You need to believe I'm the source of your misery. You need to believe we're going to fight forever. You need to believe that we can never be together.

I let you go as long as I could inside me, and I helped you be as happy as you could be. In the opposite direction, you forced yourself to believe that you were unhappy because of me. You're unhappy, but not because of me. Remember your words weeks ago: "When all those students showed me all their love for my work I felt a great emptiness inside myself and I felt a lot of pain when aware of it. I believe I started recognizing this void with you. By loving you, I recognized I had pain inside me".

Do you remember what I said to you? "It's by continuing to love beyond that pain that pain becomes love." The light always creates pain. The pain of exposure. When we expose our weaknesses, our anger, our innermost thoughts, we feel fear. Fear comes from painful experiences and pain means the beginning of death. Therefore, if what brings the light, also brings pain, the light becomes the death for that in suffering. The main purpose of life is, therefore, when we can love beyond pain. You gave me pain because you felt pain. I gave you pain because I felt pain. This cycle repeated until I stopped it inside me because I wanted to love you beyond that pain. When I did, you ran away because you felt alone in your own pain.

I'm not the one who makes you suffer. You feel pain with me for other reasons. The truth is that this negative feeling will diminish your power gradually, until you no longer feel it. At that moment, you will easily see our relationship with joy and you'll feel blessed in it. If you don't do it and keep avoiding me, one day life will put a big barrier between us and in that day, even if I want to, I can't do anything anymore. It has already begun. I lost my job here and now I only see you two days a week when I travel between cities. It could be worse, and it could be better. Your thoughts and actions promote the reality that presents us over time. If you don't want me to believe in us, the process will continue. That's how life works. What I'm doing today, again, is to help you wake up for what we have, while the time is on our side. If you can't see it, I'm so sorry... and goodbye! It's been eight months to accept that you love me. How much longer and pain do you need to accept that you want to love me?"

We Can't Stay Where We're Not True

Already working in a new city, although only a few hours away from Bianca by train, I knew about the chance she could come to work at the same university where I was.

At first she seemed motivated by the idea, despite the relationship still being quite unstable, but then invented the excuse that for heart reasons couldn't go with me.

I found out later that this was a lie. She was literally avoiding sharing a house with me. Perhaps because of fear that our discussions would increase. Still, this separation she was rising was for me very painful to witness. Shortly thereafter, she began telling me that she would work in Libya and that we wouldn't see each other for a year, or perhaps forever. She told me she wanted to be closer to France, to visit the country frequently, even a boy she was supposed to have married with, although she was no longer thinking of marrying him.

Later I made it clear how I felt and thought of her decision, after telling me that we should only maintain a friendship at the distance without future perspective:

"Bianca, suddenly, everything made sense. And even if all the people, including you, told me that I was dating a crazy woman, to me, there's no insanity without a logic that created it and can do the opposite, bringing sanity back. This logic was missing, to associate all the pieces of the puzzle. I knew there was someone in your life, but I couldn't imagine something like what you told me. I didn't want to believe it, but it all made sense. All this time, even if you didn't say it, your whole behavior proved that it would be true, including when I looked in your eyes and asked the truth about why you wanted to go to Libya and you lied with your whole body and the smallest of your muscles. Before your heart attack, you had plans to move to France and get married. With ten seconds in the world of the dead, everything changed, so you needed to think about your life. For that, you moved to a very cold place, Changchun. What you didn't expect was to fall in love with someone else, i.e. me. And since you still had plans to get married, you rushed to stop everything the next day. The confusion of feelings made you stand in the middle, undecided, and the need to hide has made you create trouble to keep me away from you. You needed excuses to leave, because your feelings wouldn't let you do it. You needed proof that I was a bad person to clean up the guilt conscience you felt. For that, you've tried everything, and for ten months, many reasons have been taken into consideration to analyze my reaction. I was too good, as far as you didn't get a slap after you gave me so many kicks. This has made you completely mad, as you increased the amount of guilt inside you, not just for what you did to someone else, but from what you were now doing to this new one. And with this, the heart problems came back and death knocked on your door again. Yes, you see, when you hurt a man of peace, you hurt yourself with a disease. It is the will of the soul, to leave a body with guilt, to leave a mind disturbed by grief. You can call it destiny, but there's no destiny without a path. Now you need Libya to get away from two people and visit the one you haven't seen in a while, because he's the one who's waiting for you. Meanwhile, you're not sure, so you need me to wait for you too. Maybe going out with other men is normal for you, maybe being away from the person you love too. But in doing that you destroyed a future marriage.

I don't want to be the second to go through this experience and, as you did to others, I believe you can do it to me. I'm not a commodity to compare to ex-boyfriends or wait for your approval. You said one day that my love for you would change. You created that change! As you entered my life and became my world, and in ten months transformed my paradise into ruins. You can see it, as you still behave as usual. But

ILLUSION

I'm not the same, and I don't look at you like I used to. You'll never have me back with your arrogance, attitude of superiority, sensuality, or whatever you still believe that works with men in general or with me. The only way to believe in you again is to see you completely honest, but with so many lies, how can I trust you? You even told me: "I don't believe in honesty. Honesty is not good". How is it possible to build a future with someone who says this? In all the messages you sent me saying, "I hope you're okay" or "I'm worried about you" or "Goodnight David," like you did yesterday, I wish you had opened your heart and said, "I love you and I don't want to lose you", "I'm sorry for what I did, let me stay with you because you're the one I want in my life." But you can't do it! You even try to make me come to you, instead of lowering your weapons down and just knock on my door like I did for you so many times. I've given up my ego for you all the time. You can't do it for me. But in your selfishness, you expect me to do it all the time. I know more than you, but I don't use it when I want to believe in someone. That's why I don't look in your eyes when you lie. That's why, as you keep lying so much, I stopped looking at your eyes. I want to believe you.

I gave you ten months of my love. You used it without any consideration for my feelings or respect for me. You remembered me only in your loneliness and you put me out of your life whenever you felt like it. You don't show any respect for life or me as a person.

I believe in a universal truth, I believe in honesty, I believe in eternal love and I believe in utter bliss. I believe that life has given you a second chance, but you are too cloistered within your pride and selfishness to see it. Go to Libya and save money for your wedding! Marry the one who's brave enough to wait for you so long! He will give you the happiness you can endure. You won't see me again. I gave myself to the strongest feeling in the world, with the less careful person to hold it. I wish you the best! I wish you happiness! I won't wait for you like the others in your life, but I will remember you forever."

After my silence had been endured for several days, and seeing that contrary to what happened before, no longer I sought her, Bianca sent me an email seeking to get me back:

"David, I know what's happening to you and I know that it's mostly my fault. You have no desire to return to this relationship because you made every effort to let me go. Maybe it's not what you really wanted, as I hurt you many times, but because the feelings still existed, you let yourself go. But the truth is, now you don't feel any more joy with me and you don't feel safe. Here are the facts: We still have problems, but I do behave differently. I try to confront my fears, speak to you, express what is wrong,... I know and I understand that at the moment and perhaps for a long period, it could be as perfect as you wish it is, that you would always expect the worst of me. Of course, I am extremely sad about your reactions, because I thought that in changing, you would also change, and you would be more affectionate and sympathetic. But I also understand your behavior and I can't blame you because it's normal. Maybe you need to take time for yourself, see if you really want to get into this relationship again. I said, and I proved that I want to build a relationship, but this time you're the one who's going to have to make some effort too. You know I love you but that doesn't mean I want to force you to believe me. You have the choice to deal with me, love me and trust me or, because of what happened in the past and in a recent past between us, you don't want or you can't anymore. I don't want us to get lost in this relationship (if it exists). If you believe in it, I will go on my way to express myself more honestly to you. If you feel you can't now, I don't think you'll be able to do it in the future, because you won't have any evidence of my behavior, as I will be away from you. Whatever you feel about me, I will respect your decision, because I care about you, and I will accept what you think is best for you. If this is a vengeance to understand where I have failed, I will accept it as well with all my affection for you."

The Goodbye

I decided to move away from Bianca forever and take a new course in my life, refusing my second job in China to look for a third, in a city as far away from her as possible. Otherwise, I knew this situation would never change, and she would always look for me when I was away, something I still couldn't resist because I had strong feelings for this woman. Bianca, for reasons she never explained to me, gave up Libya, and opted to work in the center of China, in Dalian. But for me it was the same, I was tired of her games and I had already decided to abandon her. There was nothing more to say.

Now realizing that I was ready to let her go and seeing that no longer pursued her, no longer asked for the relationship, no longer tried to talk to her, Bianca began to feel desperate. She tried to talk to me countless times, but I'd turn my phone off. She tried to come to me outside the house, but I didn't give her the liberty she had before. I was no longer interested in the relationship, as much as I loved her. She, in turn, always came out of my apartment in tears, knowing that she couldn't get the power she had before over my emotions.

It had been weeks like this. She went out on the street every time she saw me, and walked by me hoping I'd go after her, but I never did. Her manipulation and seduction games were no longer resulting. Sometimes I really came out in the morning and at night to run, the only strategy I had to overcome the pain of losing this relationship, and would be seeing her in the window looking at me, in a sadness of those who lost something important that never knew how to value. But for me nothing was justifying going back to her, and her manipulations merely nourished my bitterness. After all, I didn't intend to keep remorses about what happened.

I gave her the opportunity to go out together to say goodbye to each other, and she made an amazing effort to please me. I've never seen such a thing before. She was acting perfectly and knew how to do it. But for being something so new, also seemed a lot like artificial. I waited to see what else she was going to do and, after three days of pretending, she couldn't take it anymore and pressed me: -Do you still love me or not?

-That's not a question to ask!, I answered, feeling that this question was no longer important. But she continued to press and repeat herself, from what, already disturbed, I answered her: -You've been faking the last few days and now you're demanding something you destroyed? No, I don't love you!

That said, she left in tears, but not without before launching a new provocation to avenge herself: -I had work for you, for us to be together, but if you don't love me, I don't want to see you anymore!

I was tired of all the lying, and this provocation just worsened even more what I ever felt about her. So when she came out crying, I threw hard words on her phone by message and later by email:

"Bianca, you have no idea what love is, and then you blame others for what you do. A manipulation in which you despise another person without any consideration. You can't ask me, "Do you love me or not?" I spent several months with a person who said she didn't love me. I loved you with all my heart, without waiting for anything and respecting you, even if I knew you loved me and you were too afraid to admit it. You want me to say "I love you" after three days, after I loved you for ten months until you killed all the emotions in me. You can't even respect my feelings or take over your responsibilities in the situation. Just demands, demands, demands... You believe that everyone exists to serve you and even love should be available when you want. It doesn't work that way. You can write on a paper you want love in your life and it will come as it came. But it's your responsibility to keep it and feed it. What you did was the opposite. You had a person loving you with all his heart and eyes on you and you fought to kill all this. Now you're demanding that love come back just because you want it. No, it won't! You have to make it grow again from the root of the enormous tree you destroyed, hoping it will grow again.

Yes, it takes a lot of time and patience. It's much easier to destroy, even if this tree was so big and strong that it took ten months to finally be sent down. With all your manipulations and lies, with all the breaks you've created, the pain has transformed my brain in a way that I can't tell you but it's today much easier to overcome than you could possibly imagine.

I gave you all my love, with all my heart, and my life. While you put me out and said "I don't love you," I was loving you and in a deep pain like I never felt before. I chose not to stop loving you, so, life, to protect me, did what nature should do, changed my nature and transformed me. Love for you died in the way it existed at the beginning. You decided your whole life, you picked a new job, mailed your stuff and cleaned your house, and in the end you wanted to take me with you like I was some kind of furniture. You've put me in the last place all the time and you still do it. You planned your life without me. I don't feel the need to go after you anymore. Thanks to everything you've done. You've completely disrespected me, you said the worst things that you can tell a person who loves you, you've put me out of your life dozens of times, you said you don't love me a hundred times, you made me suffer for loving you. So here's the result! From the David who wanted you back all the time, while you said "No, no, no"... I became the apathetic David who doesn't care anymore. So, the fights you make just work on you.

There are things you do that are very evil and that I would never do. I'd come to your house and say, "I love you, and I want to be with you. I'd be happy if you took this job I found in Dalian, even though we're not together, because I love your company, and I'll continue dreaming until the day we're together again." Instead, you used this as a gambling card. And at the end, it's like you say, "You don't say what I want, so I'm going to make you feel pain: Look, I had this for you! I won't give it to you now!"

This is very sad, because it makes you look very selfish and rude. It makes it look like you tried to manipulate me and also proves that you're always trying to control me and punish me. More than that, you're vindictive with the person you should be worried about the most. I would never avenge myself on you. It's sick to even think about it! There are things in you that I would never do because they are not in my nature.

I would never repeat your behaviors to make you feel the pain you made me feel. I would never manipulate you to see if you trust me or not, among many other things you do. By making me feel anger (when you diminish me with your psychological aggression) and pain (when you expel me out of the relationship) all the time, you made me a very sad person. No wonder I didn't smile as before. You want a miracle now? Don't ask me! Pray! I hope you can find your happiness and, if possible, the man of your dreams! If, as you say, I'm the only one who made you react like that in a relationship, it shouldn't be hard to find someone who can react to you normally, and in this way, help you be happy. I wish you the best, with all the love a friend can give."

After this, I felt guilty and tried to talk to her personally, but when I walked into her house, I came across an unusual madness. Bianca had written my negative phrases sent by cellphone in small pieces of paper she glued on the door to look at all the time. Apparently, she was trying to overcome the fact of loving me, by looking at those words every time I passed through the door.

I stopped for a moment and looked at the door like the one who observes an art object. I was stunned by this woman's insane creativity. Then I started talking in a friendly tone with her while apologizing, to what she reacted with aggression. So I changed the tone of voice and the attitude, and decided to leave her alone. Maybe she realized she was ridiculous, because later she called me to talk to me, and when I got to her apartment, I didn't see the papers at the door. Actually, minutes of conversation later, we were kissing again, and soon afterwards we argued again too.

Knowing that she could lose me forever and very soon, tried to talk to me for six days, in a victim's posture, always crying and seeking to plead for my love, while saying that she loved me. But when I tried to talk to her, as always, she reversed the behaviors.

"David, I know you care about me, but you don't love me. I'm sorry we have to finish our relationship like this, but this goes beyond my strength for the moment, even though I'm being very well cared for. I don't hate you, but my body and my heart are hurting and I'm doing my best to be able to follow the road.

Since I'm very young, I wished to find the man of my dreams, because I needed him for being weak. That's why I changed and became like a robot, so I could wait. But thanks to this relationship, I realized I don't need anyone to take care of me, as to need someone is to give this person our power of life and that's wrong. Tomorrow I'm going to dream again, no matter what people can say, I'm going to dream of an ideal person who can share the rest of his life with me, but this time I'm not needy anymore. This is not to make you feel bad but to give you a piece of advice you can also use in your own life."

On the eve of leaving for another city, Bianca regretted it again and, as I didn't open the door, left gifts, which included, among other things, an MP3 player with romantic music that she said on a note to be the list of songs she made telling the story of our relationship.

Given this gesture of attention, I went to talk to her. But when our hands were together, we couldn't resist and our lips touched again.

When Illusions Stop Our Life

I was living with Bianca now, and perhaps afraid of losing me definitively, she was being thoughtful, but not very, as soon started the usual abuses. During the last days before the trip, she wanted to walk with me a lot, to say goodbye to the city, and in these walks, she showed me all the places I didn't know and that she hid from me, namely gardens and restaurants where she had walked and stayed with her college Barnabas and other friends as well as other foreign teachers. The pain I felt as she did it was unbearable. She was showing me all the places where she had fun with other men, whenever she walked away from me. And, perhaps in her own ignorance, she said, when we sat at the table of a diner for lunch, and while looking at a ring that she had on the finger: -No one ever offered me a wedding ring!

I just didn't answer. I found it totally unreasonable, abused and ridiculous, all this arrogant and presumptuous attitude. But after this, already in the garden, the arguments finally started, all because I criticized the fact that she speaks of matters in which she doesn't believe in particular, that she contradicts herself when she says she believes in spirits but doesn't believe in life beyond death. -So, in that way, you just believe in insanity!, I told her, already with my patience exhausted. Our discussions were always ridiculous and this was just another one.

The next morning things were still bad between us, but instead of finishing the relationship, she decided to invite people to her house because she knew I don't like pretending to be happy when I'm not, and I would avoid being at home with these people. But I was also tired of these games and, as a colleague had left his home key in a shoe at the door when he went traveling, in case I needed it, I used it that night.

When Bianca finished talking with one of her students, she called me over and over again, but I wasn't willing to answer her. Tired, I was already sleeping in my neighbor's bed when she came to knock on the door. I opened, and without big arguments, she asked me to go with her. But when I took the key of my friend's house, her attitude reversed: -You better stay here, because if you go with me I won't be able to sleep!

This psychological game irritated me deeply, so I told her a few truths that she needed to hear. And with this, the relationship was again finalized. But not for long, as always. Bianca would try again to approach, and also finish it, this time with a scene of screaming in the street and while sending a glass to the floor like a spoiled brat. It seemed that the fact that the separation was coming, tormented her deeply, but her torments were transformed into hatred against me. I left her at that moment when she cried and wept pathetically and took a taxi to get to our house before her. I took my suitcases and moved them to my friend's house. When she arrived, at night, was calmer and wanted to make peace with me, although the situation was still quite unstable, because the next day we would have to catch the train to Dalian, this, if I were with her of course.

She purposefully offered her apartment to a couple of friends, who moved in the moment, to prevent me from letting her go alone. And at the end, at the opportune time, hours before taking the taxi to the train station, launched the final provocation: -If you come with me, you come as a friend, because I don't want this relationship anymore and after our holidays everything will be over!

-As a friend, I won't go!, I told her to see what she was going to answer next.

-So you can give the keys of my apartment to my neighbors, because I'm going alone!

I threw the keys on the floor, called her a moron and machiavellian, and walked out the door. And, just an hour later, she called me apologizing and asking to talk to me. I went to her just to say goodbye, but she said once more she was sorry and asked if I wanted to go with her. -As a friend, I'm not going. If the relationship has to end, it ends here and today!, I told her to provoke her.

-Then I'll go alone. Goodbye!, She told me arrogantly.

ILLUSION

Half an hour before she took the taxi, called me to say goodbye one more time. I went to her apartment for the alleged goodbyes, but she wanted to talk on the street. As we walked quietly, she gave me her hand. And at that moment I told her: -Even though you were a special person to me, I'm hurt with everything that happened, but I wish you'd be happy!

Realizing I was determined not to travel with her, she began to insist, but I insisted on my viewpoint, saying it didn't make sense.

Meanwhile, the taxi to fetch her arrived and she begged me to go with her, now in tears. I kept telling her it wasn't possible and it was time to end it, and I insisted that she leave. But Bianca refused. I suggested accompanying her to the taxi, but she insisted she wouldn't go. She sat on a rock in front of me and said she wasn't able to leave. So I insisted again: -Go away, even if I have to send you by force! You're leaving!

I ended up raising my voice in a harsh tone: -Go!

Faced with this strong affirmation, she stood up and walked towards the taxi, but, meters ahead, stopped and turned back: -I'm not going without you! I love you!

-I could only go with you if we had a normal relationship and you could promise to do everything you can to stay with me!, I told her, already confused and not knowing what to think. Yes, I believed that this time, in the strength of the emotions, she could be honest, and Bianca obviously promised once more to behave like a normal person.

The first signs that I had done a mistake started right in the taxi on the way to the train-station: -Are you sure this is what you want?, she asked.

I had a deep and strong feeling that I shouldn't be inside that taxi, but the feelings for her were still strong. I was risking losing again, as usual. On the other hand, by saying goodbye to her house, I realized that this place showed me that we always bring with us what we built in our hearts. I was bringing from this house what I had manufactured there, a vast array of experiments. It was as if space symbolized a tunnel of emotions, a darkness of many trials, where instinct and emotion take control. It was like a house of dreams not belonging to the real world, a housing that existed only and especially for us, and that transformed itself, as the relationship accompanied this transformation.

Where we recover

The train trip went fast and the relationship with Bianca was transforming as we were going out of the city where we were during all our experience. And already at home of our former colleague Peppe, now living in Dalian, Bianca was different. Maybe because she was on the lookout for a third element, kept her sober posture, her usual public appearance, and didn't provoke.

This peaceful state couldn't last long, as usual. On the second day we started another discussion for ridiculous reasons. I'd hurt myself on a finger when carrying our suitcases and, while we were holding hands, she was touching that finger, so I tried to stop her hand. But she kept insisting, so I had to tell her: -Stop hurting my finger!

-Why are you yelling at me?, she asked immediately while letting go.

-I'm not shouting, but just warning that my finger is sore and, when you touch it, it hurts!, I responded in calm and serious tone. But Bianca didn't like my attitude and sulked. She separated from me, put her hands in her pockets and began to weep alone, hiding behind her glasses so that no one would notice.

Since I didn't do anything wrong, I ignored her in her childish attitude. And, shortly afterwards, she was telling me again that she didn't love me and I shouldn't have gone with her on the trip.

I told her I'd go away so there was no more trouble. I was tired of her stupid, childish and neurotic behaviors, and her lack of respect for my decision to travel with her. Beaten by emotional fatigue, upon arrival at Peppe's apartment, I started packing to leave. But when Bianca realized I was leaving, she radically changed her speech: -Don't go!

-I'm not who you want me to be, and I'm tired of seeing you complain about me all the time!, I told her, while ready to leave for good.

Before the persistence of my speech and attitude of leaving, without accepting excuses, Bianca took my two hands and begged again while trembling: -Please don't go!

-I have no more strength to endure these behaviors of yours! I shouldn't have come! I'm tired of everything you've done to me for a year and I can't stand to see you suffer and complain about me! I'm not who you want, I'm not the one who makes you happy, so I'd rather go away than keep seeing you in tears all the time!

Bianca stopped crying at this instant and, in a tone of voice altered from weak to strong, said: -I'll be strong for both! I can do it! You're the one I love! You're the one I want in my life! You don't need to make any effort! I'll do everything, but please stay!

I gave her this opportunity without high expectations and, during the next few days, she made a huge effort to keep me close, always afraid I would buy the plane ticket to leave. She was very affectionate and loving all the time and no more complained of anything. She sounded like someone else.

The Acceptance of What Cannot Change

Bianca thought of being alone with me to correct our relationship, so we ended up going to a hotel away from Peppe.

The arrival at the hotel was promising. The relationship was more stable, but not for long. After a few constant discussions, the argument that would take us away finally occurred at the end of a lunch. -Here's on this paper all the money you owe me! Also includes the taxi. I don't need to, but as you are stingy, I wanted to include everything in the smallest detail!, Bianca said, while showing a paper with all this information counted.

-Do you really think I'm stingy?, I questioned her, trying to understand the true intent of the question.

-Yes, I think!, she responded firmly.

-Oh, yes?, I asked her again in a serious tone, hoping she'd awaken to the stupidity of her assertion. But she insisted...

-Yes, I do!

-Okay!, I answered without arguing. Her stupidity was over me, because in reality that lunch was the first time she paid whatever it is. For a whole year, I've always been paying for both of us.

-I'm sorry I called you a stinger!, said Bianca afterwards, realizing that I was troubled. And then continued to insist on controlling the situation: -Why are you like this if I said I was sorry?

-I'm hurt and I don't feel like talking, but I'm here with you!

-If you want to leave, we can meet later!

I didn't go and Bianca stayed with me. We ended up in a café, and she didn't say anything, waiting for me to say something. But I felt tired of her behaviors, so she started crying: -Why don't you say something?

-I have nothing to say!

-You don't love me! You've been faking it for me, even in the way we make love!

I got deeply irritated with the insinuation: -During the first six months of the relationship you couldn't even say you loved me! You hurt me in many ways for a year and now you're questioning me if I love you?

Bianca started crying even more, while rising to go away: -I'm going to the hotel! Anytime you want, come meet me for us to leave!

However, I remained in the same place to rest my head of this insanity for another hour.

When I arrived at the hotel, we took the suitcases to return to Peppe's house. We were going in silence, when she started to slowdown the pace to test my reaction. I stood up to wait her, until she finally said something: -Why do you hurt so much?

-I don't do anything to you, but I don't think I'm the man you want!, I said. And the more she was whining, the more I reaffirmed the same phrase: -I'm not the man you want!

-I'm not going with you! I'm staying at the hotel for more days! You go alone!, She replied angrily.

Tired of her immaturity, I opened my backpack to give what belonged to her and then followed the path alone.

Already at Peppe's house, who meanwhile knew what was going on, I found she wouldn't stay at the hotel in the city centre, but on the contrary, she was on her way. I thought she gained consciousness of her behaviors and would come to me, but it wasn't the case. She stayed at a hotel near Peppe's house.

For the next few days, she hoped I would apologize, which never happened, because I had nothing to say to her. I was tired of apologizing for something that wasn't really my fault. During the next five days, Bianca went to her friend's house when I was not present and left me messages in the bed. But the messages were always very aggressive: -Go away! It's all over for me!

I also knew that she had asked Peppe the exact date and time when I was going to get on the plane to leave. So I asked Peppe not to tell her, in order not to prolong these ridiculous games. And, meanwhile, Bianca decided to send me an email:

"David, our last written conversation through Peppe's hands and words gave me more grief than anything I've endured this year. I left you in Dalian because I couldn't stand the fact that you didn't love me anymore, that you were pretending that our relationship was depending on my behavior. Yes, I was sad to see your anger, your sadness, your indifference to my feelings, to my joy in being with you, my love for you, my body, my mind,... Yes, I left you because I understood you lied to me, that everything I could do was not and would never be enough. Yes, I left you to feel good with someone who could hear you and give you the hospitality you need. You made me pay the price of giving you grief, you made me see that I was nothing like the others because I couldn't love you as you are. Since you weren't able to write a few words for me, you showed me that I didn't deserve to be with you. And what can I say? Maybe you're right. Once again I'd like to apologize for the pain I gave you, because I can't love you like you wanted to. I'd like to apologize for not having the level you want me to have. I forgive you for my grief, for the guilt you gave me."

The next day she went to talk to Peppe and crossed with me several times, but I ignored her, because I had already purchased the plane ticket, and the last thing I needed at that time was more emotional torture. But, Bianca called me later, after a few hours, through an unidentified number, to make sure that I answered the call: -It's just to say that I'm going to get the rest of my stuff in the morning. Even though you lied to me and you don't love me, I hope you're there to give me what I want! You can leave it at the door! It's the least you can do, since you're enjoying his house!

I ignored her, because that morning I took the plane to Guangdong, but I left her a long farewell letter in the hands of Peppe, a letter I considered as the last one, because I didn't want to see her anymore:

"I've loved you like I've never loved anyone in my entire life. You helped me find happiness in life and meanings to live. I wanted to get married as soon as possible and start creating a life with you. I was ready to have children with you, build a dream and bring it to reality. But, as you stated at the beginning of the relationship, I was choking you with my love. Then you started rejecting my love in many different ways. Every one of them as painful as if someone was ripping off the best part of me. My heart suffered the attack of many arrows, your harshest words:

-I don't love you;
-Soon this love will disappear;
-All my ex-boyfriends were better than you;
-You make me unhappy;
-I don't trust you;
-You're violent and aggressive;
-I lied to you, I don't care about you and I never loved you;
-You destroyed my love for you;
-You're not the man I want in my life;
-I'd rather have a simple life than have love;
-I'd rather have a loving man than a passionate man like you;
-You're immature. I want a real man;
-Your help hurt me;
-I look like a living dead because of this relationship with you;
-This relationship is making me sick;
-Like mine, your love for me will turn into something else.
-We will both find someone to love and that is the best for us;
-If I stay with you, I will be unhappy all my life;
-You are diabolical;
-You're bad;
-You're a liar;
-You're greedy;
-You're weird;
-You're stupid;
-You're violent;
-I will always hurt you, and I will never change;
-I don't believe in this relationship anymore;
-I will be happy but not with you;
-I want you to find someone else to love.

Physical violence was also a great arrow in my chest. Especially when you said you did it because of my words.

Bianca, if you think that physical violence is excusable, you should question those who were aggressive with you in the past for their reasons, because I am sure that all people have their own motives! You were never happy with me, no matter what I did. The reasons for your rejection have always been different:

-You don't care about me;
-You're not romantic;
-You have no interest in my life;
-You're too centered on yourself;
-You don't care about my troubles.

I understand that at the end of all this, you tried to alter your behavior, but couldn't. You've been hiding the lies and the manipulations. The whole experience in this relationship has become something else, certainly, as you predicted when saying: "Our love will become something else as soon as I leave you".

My love for you has become an act of compassion instead of a gift of love, as my pain has transformed into knowledge and the relationship has formed in wisdom. Throughout the experience I've had with you, I've been able to create the ideal man's profile for you, which I will never be. And that's why I told you: "I'm not the person you want to love". These are the characteristics of the person you want to love:

Rich – You've often said you need lust;

Stupid – If he's stupid, he won't be able to see your manipulation techniques, such as "Thanks to me you're happier", "Thanks to me you're not having a miserable vacation," "I always know what's best for you," "I don't eat because of you," "I don't sleep because of you". He won't be able to see that your control in a relationship, a control that you need because you cannot truly love anyone without fears, is always based on the same strategy: The guilt and self-respect of others associated with a dependency on your actions. He will not be able to see that you take his happiness into your world, and then control him by making him feel that you're the source of that happiness;

Non-artist – artists are too sensitive. They feel the pain too much. So you need someone who's not so "susceptible" and "sensitive" as you usually say. You need someone whom you can hurt without any remorse, as you can't manage other people's pain, especially if you're responsible for it;

Low self-esteem – As you need to complain about your partner's behavior and his actions, without any reproaches in return, the only way to feel perfect in your behavior is to live with someone without self-esteem, so you can complain without any feedback;

Independent - You need a man who doesn't need you. Because in this sense you can do whatever you want without having to justify or ask first. You can say goodbye and disappear altogether whenever you want and be accepted whenever you come back. You can say "I don't want to see you anymore" and stop seeing him for weeks until you miss him, for purely sexual reasons or not. And if you're just homesick for sexual issues, you can use him as a hooker and say goodbye the next day just like you did me;

Caring – You need a man who presents daily physical evidence of his love so you can believe that you are beloved. He should give you flowers, bracelets, earrings, rings, etc. Otherwise you won't trust his love. Words have no impact on you unless they carry pain. So I could say "I love you" for a whole year and you would never believe it;

Naive – Because every time you say "let's forget the past" he will be able to do it, believe you, and then you can hurt him again exactly in the same way you always did;

Older - Because you will not be ashamed to present him to your friends, colleagues, or students. If he's older, you won't tell him that he's immature, you won't disrespect him, and you won't behave like you're superior because he's going to have more life experience;

What I saw at first, when I met you, was very obvious. And it is a fact that if you are afraid of loving, you'll give pain to all those who love you, as you believe that they can hurt you. By hurting them, you hurt yourself and create your own cycle of strengthening a personal belief. In psychology this is called a self-fulfilled prophecy. I still see in you the little girl I saw at the beginning, holding a huge shield to protect the heart in one hand and a huge sword in the other hand, pointing to all those who try to touch your fragile heart. This is your karma, a pride developed to protect you from humiliation. It was the fear that created all these qualities that formed your personality and trapped you in your own creation, your armor. The less love you have, the more admiration you need. But you refuse love by focusing on the need to be admired. Dishonesty is a trap that holds you in your mental certainties, which have no connection to reality, even though you expect others to believe in them. You followed your pride instead of love, but true love is not selfish.

The love you couldn't accept began to kill you. When I saw your face turning into a death image, when I saw you in a pain that made you so weak that you couldn't stop crying and feel the worst person in the world, when I saw that you could kill yourself because of me, when I saw all this, I gave up. In this love I'll let you go. Today I turn the page of my life. Tomorrow I start a new life.

As I see your words before I go, listen to your voice on the phone, see your messages written on the paper or observe your behaviors, I can tell you that it is true what you say: you will never change. Please be happy! And may all your wishes be fulfilled! You will always be my little angel."

Bianca's response to my unexpected departure followed shortly:

"David, when arriving yesterday at my temporary apartment, I felt the need to offer it to you. While others could see it as an old place on top of an old building, I see it as a gift, because it was destined to be ours. The apartment number is 151, it's old but it's big, with a terrace, and is located behind the park where we spent the last few days together. I'm not trying to play you or make you suffer. What I'm saying is that, since I got here, I'm enjoying it as if you're here with me. I've been through, since we've separated, hours in grief, being jealous of Peppe, being able to give you what you expect to receive, crying, thinking about you all day and waiting for a sign of you. Maybe Peppe has a point in explaining that it's best not to see each other again, because I can just hurt you and we're separated today. But like you, I'm capable of listening to others and not care about what they think. And that's probably why we couldn't trust our relationship. I wish I could understand your language and have been able to fill your lack of confidence with my love for you. But I felt it. Even though I know you don't love me anymore, that you're hurting, that you'd rather be in another place than with me, I just wanted to say goodbye properly to you. So, as I am stubborn, I take my right without asking permission to say goodbye to the man I love and who has made me experience and discover so much about myself this year. As you are every day more and more conscious of your responsibilities, you now take back your power in life and show yourself and the world that you are strong, fearless, and loving.!No matter how far, time or age, my heart is always with you!"

During the next five days, she spent her time crying and suffering from the fact that I left. She'd send me e-mails all the time and messages to my cellphone. She was telling me to have courage, that she would be with me all the way, that she loved me, etc. After four days, she began to realize I could no longer go back to her and, therefore, the messages she sent were now pleading for me to speak to her.

Finally, I decided to take one of her calls: -Despite everything you wrote in the letter and what you feel, I love you!, said Bianca, although she didn't seem very interested in the idea of having me visiting her.

However, I was still not prepared to end the relationship, although I would think so. I ended up catching a plane to visit her. I closed the door to my new apartment and took a little suitcase prepared in a hurry with some clothes.

Being Authorized to Live

Bianca was anxiously waiting for me at at the airport from an early time. What we felt was still very strong and we embraced when I arrived. But at the same time, I could not fail to feel a deep pain in the heart, knowing that she had preferred to have her coworker, with whom she was always spending the day, as her colleague again in the new job and city. It was also difficult to endure the fact that few efforts she made to spend the few days I had with me. Not only would she rather be with her colleague, as she insisted that I go with them. The arguments were several, like: "Poor guy, he is alone"; "I need to talk to him about the lessons," or even, "he's going to show us the town."

Whatever the argument was, seeing her repeat the same attitude, after catching a plane on purpose to see her, it was too overwhelming. I didn't want to spoil the moment and I had a lot to handle But the last shred of patience vanished from me, when on the last day before I left, when recording songs that she offered, I discovered my files on her computer. I was stunned by seeing a lot of personal files she had stolen from me. I found out that she had copied important e-mails that I exchanged with other people, e-mails that included, for example, conversations with ex-girlfriends. But she also copied all my books and information about personal projects. And I realized that her only intention was to get enough information to manipulate me more efficiently and not to understand me as a person. I was upset, but as I was going to get on the plane, I didn't tell her anything.

Being Accepted

After my arrival to Guangdong, I received the invitation to change to a new apartment, much larger than the previous one, with a balcony and view to the mountains. By closing the door of the previous apartment, I got the odd feeling that this apartment had a double function: Healing a broken heart and enabling an emotional transformation. One way or another, with or without travel to Dalian, more properly Lushun, that apartment had fulfilled the task of receiving my pain. And the new apartment would serve a new state of mind, which couldn't be achieved without clearing the emotions with the help of another space.

Bianca would call me every day, saying she missed me, but the hypocrisy of her words would let me feel very bad about myself. Besides, I wouldn't allow myself the same liberty to call back. She said all the time she didn't have time to talk to me and could only write. So I ended up deciding to eliminate her contact, prohibiting her from contacting me. From there, Bianca began to leave messages that she had come to the internet on purpose to talk to me and that she had spent the last few days thinking of me. But my patience had long crossed the boundaries and I wrote to her:

"The person who cares about you, will try to understand you, and in that effort, will see your mistakes. You ask a lot without giving in return. I'm not an idiot, and I'm not going to close my eyes to your attitudes just because you need it. Amazingly, you've shared more time with Barnabas than with me. I still wonder why... After all the efforts I've made for our relationship to work, I know you will try to keep this love at distance for I don't know how much longer. I don't understand what kind of love you really want to have with me. I really don't know what to think when you say "I just wanted to hear your voice," or "even if we're not together, I need us to be friends."

I wonder if you really want a relationship with me. After planning your escape, questioning why I stopped believing in the relationship or because I stopped trusting you. It's so obvious I wonder if you're making me look stupid. In my life, and unless I'm crazy...

-I'm not going to marry someone who can't live with me;
-I will not want to have a child with someone who can't even accept me;
-I will not share a house with someone who fights to live in secrecy;
-I will not share a business with someone who only works for her own benefit;
-I'm not going to trust someone who steals my knowledge.

I'm sure, in all the pain that love can bring, when the storm destroys its fruits, that all psychologists, psychiatrists and healthy people in this world would agree with this. It's not about you. It has to do with life itself. May the next man you love have what you couldn't give me: respect, compassion, and compromise."

On the sixth day, after sending this message, Bianca responds:

"Dear David, the purpose of this email is to help you not worry about me. I couldn't talk or write to you before, but now I'm better. I'm writing to tell you that I want to end this relationship with you. As I write this letter, I know that my whole life I will miss your sweetness. This nice, elegant, talented, intelligent young man who made me believe in love and helped me be more myself through him. But it's because of the rest I wanted, that I decided and today I chose to follow the rest of my life without you. Thank you my love for all the magic you have brought to my life, thank you for all your beautiful gifts, your beautiful smile and your laughter. I'm always here for you because I'm always thinking about you!"

This was my answer to her:

ILLUSION

"You're a cold-blooded vampire with no compassion or emotions. In your moments of agony, your mind will become clear, and you shall suffer the power of consciousness. When that happens, your heart will suffer for what you've lost. You'll have it alone until the last days of your life. Because after me, you can't risk writing on a paper again: I want love, I want the man of my dreams! And you won't be able to write again that you want to solve your karma. Because God gave you that hypothesis and you refused, as the power of consciousness was too strong for you. The day you die, you'll see what life really means. I wish I could help you see, but I don't have that power. You're a slow student, little angel, and you're too far from the truth. I gave you the light you needed in your darkness, but you're now a creature of the dark. You despise all the light, all the love and freedom of consciousness. You sucked my last drop of blood, you took the last remaining energy in me. You won! But in the day I saw you for the first time, I knew I'd lost already. The day I said "I love you", I was surrendering. And if in your life you wish to die, remember, my little angel, it's just the lack of love, not of the world, but of yourself! Goodbye! "

The Response of Consciousness

While I was revolted with everything, trying to resume my life once again, my conscience began to process a set of thoughts on subjects that had previously not been noticed. I began to realize that, most likely, Bianca was playing with several men at the same time, maintaining relationships with Barnabas and Luc, and likely even more. Yes, Bianca showed many signs of sexual addiction and need to be loved simultaneously by several men, which is characteristic of a nymphomaniac.

Although her love could be true, the need for several sexual partners was also a constant in the subconscious of this woman. All of this, facts which, despite increasingly clearer, she would never admit. After all, I began to accept the fact that she would never surrender to someone and my situation wouldn't be unique. I realized she might even want to marry and have children with me, but she couldn't really love me, because she's a very sick person from a psychological standpoint.

It was during this period that I also remembered when one day we talked about her behaviors and she said: "There is no cure for my problem but only medicine". Although she never admitted what she was talking about, she was very likely referring to the fact that she is a nymphomaniac and was already diagnosed as such by a professional psychiatrist in the past. Her refusal to take medication for the problem, corresponded to the fear of being no longer as she is, although, like any other woman, she needed to be loved and have a family, which became more important as she reached the age of forty.

As always, Bianca would try to look for me again, sending more emails, even if I never answered again, staying forever in silence.

"David, from the beginning of the relationship with you that I felt bad because everything seemed to be wrong with me, but this time you treated me the worst way you could to destroy me. First, I was very angry reading your words, but then I felt like I deserved. If a person is capable of loving me, he can write me or speak like that. I felt that I deserved to be treated like a machiavellian person and I went back to the darkest of me. I'd like to apologize if I hurt you, but I was so hurt too, due to my past, that I couldn't show love like you wanted. You're the only person in my life who knows my whole story and especially how guilty I feel for not being as good a person as I should be. As my only love, as my confidant, you should have paid attention to that! Maybe someone else didn't react the same way, but I'm not someone else. I'm not like you. I endured, darkness and pain not only for a few years David, not just for a few years... I don't want to blame you1 If you feel guilt about what happened, you don't have to feel it! I can't help but forgive you, because I forgave my past! I gave you the key to my vault so you could open it and give me my gift. Today I use that skill to write to you and speak with an open heart. So, even if I am hurt, I will always be thankful that I have met you and loved you. Remember my smiles, but not my cries. Remember, I have no regrets, not one. I wish you love, happiness and peace. I hope we'll be more careful in the next life."

"David, I know you decided not to talk to me anymore because you believe it's the best for us. I suppose you know better than me what's right. Every day I tell myself that you made the right decision because we hurt each other. But despite our struggles and hatreds, I miss you as before. I don't know if you'll receive or open this email, but I'm worried about you and I hope you're okay."

"David, I beg you to help me! I need to know if you're better off alone, wherever you are, than with me, if it's all over! I can't do our grief if you don't help me, because I can't stop thinking about us. I'll wait for your answer!"

"David, I wish we hadn't hurt each other so much, and I wish we'd been more careful. I wish we'd showed everyone what love can do, but that didn't happen. On the contrary. What I know of the mistakes, and I have a million, is that behind them there is comprehension and success. So, yes, I'm really sorry I'm not the one that's going to make you happy and dream, I am hurt to remember our past together and see our present apart, but I always wish for your happiness and I believe in a life together, even though that was not clear to you, so I hope that, no matter what happened, you're now experiencing, living and rediscovering the joy of living that you've lost with me. Tonight I have to be strong and admit my defeat. I have to let you go, even if I'm never able to get you out of my heart. Good luck, my love! Show everyone who you are and love again!"

Book Review Request

Dear Reader, Thank you for purchasing this book! I would love to know your opinion. Writing a book review helps in understanding readers and also has an impact on other reader's purchasing decisions. Your opinion matters. Please write a book review! Your kindness is greatly appreciated!

Booklist

Books written by the author:
Agne: Inside the Mind of a Narcissist
Destiny: When Your Soulmate Finds You
Disenchanted: Poems by Rowan Knight
Illusion: When a Nymphomaniac Falls in Love
One Chance: 20 Short Stories with a Plot Twist and Moral Lesson
Prophecy: A Message to Humanity
Slave: Fulfilling a Prophecy
Soulless: Letters to a Narcissist

About the Publisher

This book was published by the 22 Lions Bookstore.

For more books like this visit www.22Lions.com.

Join us on social media at:

Fb.com/22Lions;

Twitter.com/22lionsbookshop;

Instagram.com/22lionsbookshop;

Pinterest.com/22LionsBookshop.